Carolina's Courage

ELIZABETH YATES

Carolina's Courage

Illustrated by NORA S. UNWIN

NEW YORK ✓ E. P. DUTTON & CO., INC.

 Library of Congress Catalog Card Number: 64-10697. Published simultaneously in Canada by Clarke, Irwin & Company Ltd., Toronto and Vancouver. First Edition.

This is the story of Carolina Putnam and the doll that was her treasure. She loved it more than anything else in the world. She knew that she would never part with it, nor did she until — but that is the story.

FOR THE *Story Hour* CHILDREN,
TO WHOM THIS STORY WAS FIRST TOLD

Chapter one

CAROLINA LIVED with her mother and father and older brother Mark on a small New Hampshire farm in the middle years of the nineteenth century. The rounded hills that sloped gently up to the sky had been familiar to her for as long as she had been aware of her world, as had the road that wound valley-ward to the village.

In the village there was a white church with a slender spire, and to it the Putnam family went every Sunday morning. There were also a store where Carolina's father traded once a week, and a school that the Putnam children attended. But Carolina had begun to wonder how much longer she and Mark would be going to that school.

For months and months past, all during the long cold winter, her father had talked about leaving their high farm with its thin, stony soil and going west where good land could be had for the claiming and where the weather worked with a man instead of so often against him. Now that the winter days were lengthening into spring, it seemed that John Putnam could think and talk about nothing else. And always his talk ended by his saying to his wife, "I tell you, Annah, if I can get any price at all for this farm of ours, I'll buy us a wagon, and we'll be off."

One April day, when the sun shone with comforting warmth and the fields were beginning to show some signs of drying out after the heavy snows that had lain on them for the past four months, John Putnam returned from his weekly trip to the village. He was tired and hungry. The roads had been muddy, and much of the way he had walked beside the cart to save the horse.

"We'll have our supper now instead of later," Annah Putnam said, "so you can rest yourself before the evening chores."

They sat around the table in the kitchen, and John Putnam gave them the news of the village and of his day; but when his talk started to be of going west Carolina slipped away from the table and went to find Lydia-Lou.

Sitting on the door rock in the late afternoon sunshine, which was still warm though the breeze was blowing cool, Carolina placed her doll in the little cherry-wood chair that her father had made; then she told her of what had taken place at the supper table. "And Papa is saying the same thing all over again, Lyddy, that he's tired of trying to farm this stony land and wants to go west where there are no stones. Mama says she'll go, of course, but she really doesn't want to leave this house. Mark just listens and says nothing. What do you want to do, Lyddy?"

The doll's black eyes stared out of her painted-china face. Her china hands were crossed neatly on her lap; her china feet with their painted black-buttoned shoes peeped out from under her layers of petticoats.

"That's what I think too," Carolina replied. "I don't care whether we stay here or go there just as long as we can always be together." She picked Lyddy up and held her close.

The flexible sawdust-stuffed body yielded readily; the china face returned a cool kiss.

Carolina placed Lyddy in her chair again, then moved the chair back against the house and out of the way of anyone who might be coming or going. She smoothed the muslin dress with its sprig pattern of rosebuds, and leaned close to whisper a brief word of parting. "Stay there, Lyddy, like a good girl, and I'll soon be back with you." Carolina left the house and went toward the barn to be there when her father came to do the chores.

Bossie, the brown-and-white cow, was waiting patiently to be milked. Jack, the old black horse, nibbled at stray green shoots of grass. The chickens walked around looking for bugs. Carolina climbed up onto the barnyard gate, watching them all and thinking how hard it would be to leave them.

"You'll miss the farm, won't you, Carolina?"

She turned quickly to meet her father, and nodded her head.

"Never mind," he said, as he swung her up in one arm, the milk pail dangling over the other, "we'll have a much better farm in the West."

Bossie followed them into the barn and went to her stanchion. John Putnam set his daughter down in the straw near Bossie, put his stool in place and his pail under the cow's full udder, then began to milk.

Fascinated as always, Carolina watched his firm yet gentle hands on Bossie's teats. She watched the streams of milk that went into the pail, and listened to what her father had to say to her. This was always their best time together, and many a story had John Putnam told to Carolina in the length of time it took to fill the pail with milk and empty the cow's udder. But the story he told her this time was unlike any he had ever told her before.

In words that were like his hands, firm yet gentle, he put together the long conversations that had been going on in the Putnam household during the past winter, and even long before that. Mark and Carolina had often been a silent part of the conversations as they all sat around the big table in the kitchen; but there were times when the talk had continued long after the children had gone to bed. Many a night Carolina had been aware of the murmuring sound of her parents' voices rolling over her as she drowsed in the trundle bed. It was always a comforting sound because it meant that they were near, and she neither knew nor cared what they said.

By the time the cow was stripped and the pail was full and foaming at the top, Carolina knew that Bossie was to be sold, and the chickens, that old Jack was to be given to a neighbor, and that of the working animals only the two oxen would be kept. Even the house would be sold, and the land with it, and much of their furnishings, and in its place they would have a house on wheels. That was the news John Putnam had brought back from the village that afternoon.

"A house on wheels?" Carolina asked, trying to imagine what such a dwelling would be like.

"Yes. It will be a wagon with a canvas roof. Into it we'll stow everything that will be needed in our new life, as well as provisions for the journey. What we do not need we must leave behind."

"And what about Lyddy's little red chair?"

"Perhaps we shall find room in the wagon for her chair."

"And her box of clothes? And the bed you made for her? And my tea set? And —"

"You will have to choose, Carolina. Just one thing belonging to Lyddy can you take. That will be the rule for each one of us when it comes to deciding about our treasures. So much we must take — my plow, your mother's churn, bedding, clothes, tools and seeds, food, and a few small items to trade with the Indians. It will not be possible to find room in the wagon for the many things we might want to take."

Carolina stood up and brushed some of the straw from her dress, then she went over to the wall where a wooden cup hung on a peg. She took it down and handed it to her father. This was something they always did together and looked forward to. He wiped the cup against his sleeve; he dipped it in the milk. Blowing the foam away, he handed the cup to Carolina. She drank slowly from her side, handed it back to him and he drank from his. The milk was warm, and there was a sweet smell of cow to it.

"Will there be another Bossie in that far — far place?" she asked.

"Yes, someday," he assured her, "but not soon, not for a while."

Carolina looked up at her father but she could not see him clearly, for tears had come seeping into her eyes. "When do we leave?" she asked in a voice so small that she scarcely heard it herself.

"Before the month is out, as soon as our arrangements are made and the roads have dried." He stooped to pick up the pail, but before he started back to the house he put his free hand on her shoulder. "A pioneer has no time for tears, Carolina."

Carolina bit her lips together and listened until she heard her father's footsteps leave the barn. Another minute and she knew he would be nearing the house. She held her lips tight. Distantly a door swung shut. Carolina put her arms around

Bossie's neck. She pressed her face hard against the soft coat to muffle the sound, and cried.

Bossie reached into her manger for hay, munched it, turned her head sideways to see what was happening, mooed, then reached into her manger again. Jack nickered. The chickens clucked as they entered the barn and sought their night's roosting. Alone with the friendly creatures, Carolina was sure of one thing, and that was that she had not become a pioneer. Perhaps tomorrow she would be, but tonight she was a New Hampshire child, born and bred, crying for the only home she had ever known and soon would never know again.

It was almost dark when she left the barn. She stopped by the watering trough to wash her face and smooth her hair. She ran her hands down her dress to smooth away the wrinkles and remove any wisps of hay or straw. She lifted her head and saw the first star and paused long enough to wish; then she walked toward the house. Lyddy was still sitting where she had left her. Carolina picked her up just as she was, little red chair and all, and went into the house.

In the kitchen, John and Annah Putnam were standing by the table. A wooden box was open on it, and they were already starting to take things down from the shelves and stow them away in the box.

"Good night, Papa. Good night, Mama," Carolina said as she went up to each one in turn, giving and receiving a kiss.

"I'll come in to see you when you're in bed," Annah said. Her hands closed around a dish, a plain old butter dish, as if it had suddenly become precious beyond price.

John Putnam said, "Good night, Carolina," but the smile he gave his daughter told her more than any words.

Mark was kneeling by the hearth, bundling tools together and tying them with rope. Carolina watched him for a moment.

"What are you taking, Mark, that's your very own?"

He reached into his pocket and brought out a compass. "It won't use up any room because it'll always be with me and it may help us find our way. You taking Lyddy?"

"Yes."

Carolina put the cherry-wood chair down on the hearth beside the settle, then went into the next room where the big bed stood. She set Lyddy down beside the bed while she undressed and folded her clothes neatly over the blanket box; she drew out the trundle bed and knelt beside it. Lyddy was made to kneel, too, and her flexible legs accepted the position willingly.

After a few moments, Carolina got into the trundle bed and drew the quilt up over herself and Lyddy. She held the doll close to her. A house on the ground or a house on wheels, she thought, it really did not matter; it would be home if she had Lyddy in her arms.

A quarter of an hour later, when Annah Putnam went into the bedroom to tuck up Carolina, she saw that she was already fast asleep with Lyddy in her arms. Generally she took the doll away and laid her at the foot of the bed, ready for the morning; but tonight she did not do this. She stood quietly watching the two, and a wave of thankfulness surged over her that it was the doll Carolina loved, for a doll was small and could go with them all the long journey. Were it a dog or a calf, or even one of the chickens, or something they could not take, the parting would be very hard.

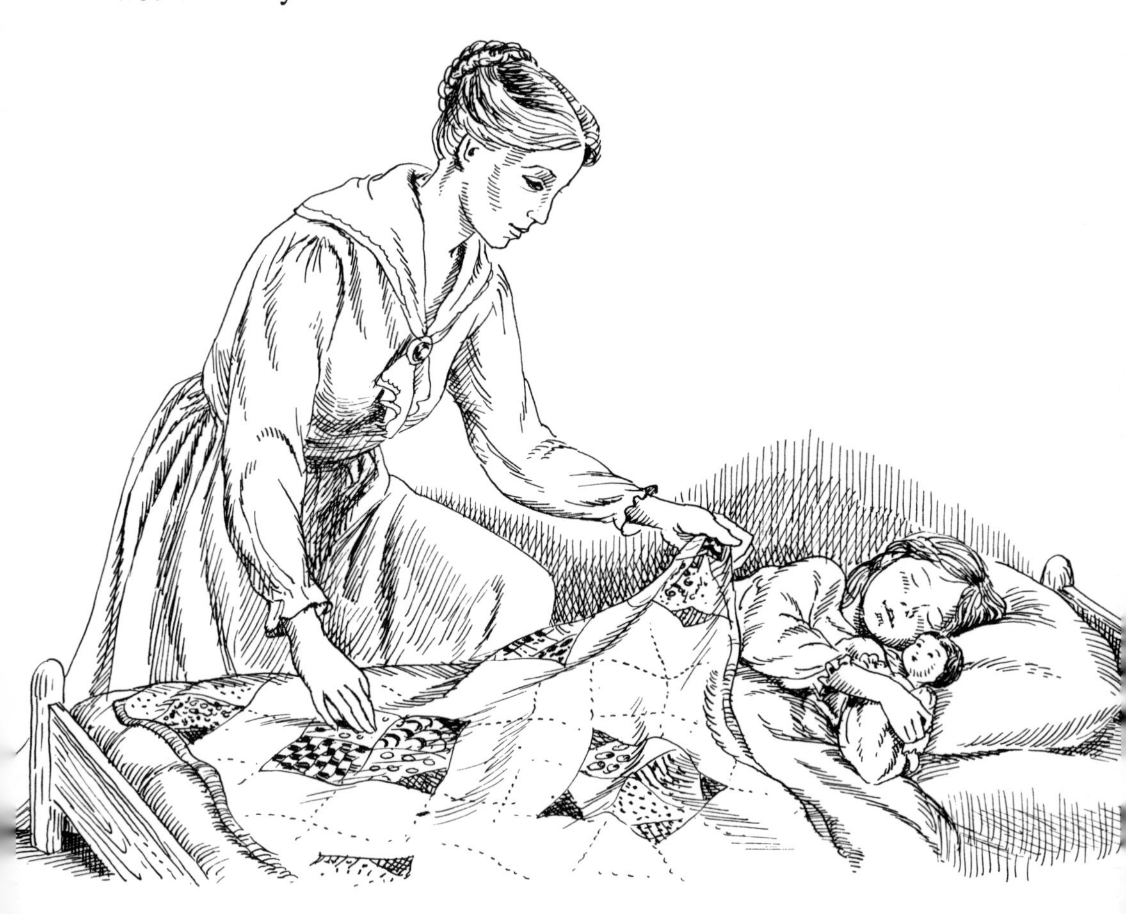

Chapter two

ALL THE TALKING that John Putnam had done during the past winter had come to reality on the April day when he received and accepted an offer for his house and land. True, it was not what the place was worth by any means; but, as he said to Annah, it was a good bargain if it enabled him to buy a wagon for the journey and have a little cash in hand. He knew of more than one man who had abandoned house and farm and gone west with his family when news of good land free for the claiming had reached New Hampshire. Fractious weather and stubborn soil were things no one wanted to struggle with all his days when there was a chance for another kind of life.

"It will be hard, John," Annah said, late that April night after the children had gone to bed.

"We're used to hardship, Annah."

"Is it a great risk we're taking, John?"

"No, no more than any living is a risk. A hundred acres can be mine for the claiming. I'll work them for five years, and then they'll be legally mine with a document to prove it. A hundred acres of black soil, deep and rich, and free of stones!"

"Isn't there anything else but soil, John?"

"There's timber, Annah, and water."

"Sounds as if you're going to have everything you've always wanted."

"I'm thinking a man can have what he wants if he's willing to work for it."

"Where is it, John, this land that has the rainbow's gold buried in it?"

"In the Nebraska Territory, Annah, that's just being opened up to settlers."

Annah looked no wiser. It was the end of the world to her. "And there's no risk," she repeated. But this time it was not a question.

"With good land beneath our feet and the sky above? We're young, Annah, and strong, and the children are growing into strength. It will be hard — I grant you that — and it will call for all that we can give, but the rewards will be great. You will see, Annah; you will see."

"It will call for something more than strength of body and skill of hand," she reminded him.

He was silent for a moment, then took her right hand in his and held it firmly. "I know, Annah. It will call for stout hearts.

Are you willing to go?"

She glanced away from him, and her gaze took in the lamp-lit kitchen, the fire on the hearth, the clock on the mantel, her loom in a corner, the slat-back chairs. Beside the settle, looking very small in the shadows, was the cherry-wood chair that John had made for Carolina's doll. All these, and so much more, her eyes took in before she turned them back to her husband. Her gaze met his.

"Yes, John. I am willing."

The next morning John Putnam went to a neighboring town to purchase a wagon for the journey. From the time that the great vehicle with its high wheels and bellying canvas top was drawn up the hill and came to rest in the Putnams' dooryard, the days that followed seemed like so many hours.

It was no less than a well-made farm wagon, four feet wide by nine feet long. Sides and ends were boarded to a height of two feet, which gave it a deep interior bed, and this bed had a removable floor that provided storage compartments for articles that would not be used during the journey. Seams were tight, for there would be times when, crossing rivers, a wagon bed might have to serve as a boat. But it was much more than an ordinary farm wagon.

Bent hickory bows supported a canvas roof that could be rolled up on the sides or fastened tight to the wagon. Flaps at either end could be opened and tied back, or the puckering strings could be drawn and the interior would be as enclosed

as a house with doors. The canvas top had been waterproofed with linseed oil and would be as sure a protection against rain as the wagon box would be against high river water. The inside of the wagon was an empty room with curving walls. In any part of it, Mark and Carolina could stand upright; but only in the center could their parents stand without stooping.

"It's as well made as a wagon can be," John Putnam said approvingly. "The running gear is light and strong, and even though the wheels are rimmed with iron the iron is light and does not add much to the weight. That tongue of hickory wood will take the oxen's yoke well. The rest of the wood looks as if it had been seasoned for years, which is as it should be, for we want no splitting axles or wheels wobbling from shrinkage on our journey."

"There are no springs that I can see," Annah remarked doubtfully.

"And no more should there be! Who ever saw springs in a farm wagon?"

"Hay is one thing, John, people and their possessions quite another."

"But the journey is what matters. Light and strong and watertight, that's how this wagon was built."

Mark came clambering down from the seat after his inspection. "There's no brake, Pa. Did they forget to put one on the wheels?"

"There are no brakes on these wagons, son."

"What's to happen when we go down a hill? What's to keep the wagon from riding over the oxen?"

"We lock a rear wheel with a chain at the crest of a hill. That holds the wagon as well as a brake, and it means less weight."

Carolina had been sitting on the front seat with Lyddy in her arms. She started to climb down, but her father called to her to stay where she was.

"You shall have the first ride, Carolina. Wait there till I bring up the oxen. It will do them good to get used to the wagon, even though it may feel like an eggshell to them."

In another few minutes the oxen were yoked to the wagon tongue, and John Putnam led them out into the field. Carolina sat on the seat, happy and proud, with Lyddy on her lap. Before her was the familiar field, behind her the empty space of the wagon. It seemed so big, as if everything in house and barn could be stowed away in it; but as the days went on and the wagon was slowly filled with their possessions, she felt less sure that it could hold all they needed to take.

The sun shone warm and strong during those April days. Snow that had lain close to the house disappeared. Only on the north side of the barn and in deep shadowy places in the woods was any snow left. There were still soft spots on the roads, and some mudholes, but the ground was drying rapidly and firming up. The Putnams would not be the first to travel the road with a wagon bound for the West. Already two families had come down from farther north and had gone through the village, walking beside their loaded wagons. No need to ask them where they were going. There was only one direction these days: west.

"When will we be on our way, Pa?" Mark asked every morning. Now he, as his father, had only one thought in his mind.

"Soon. In another week the roads will be that much drier. The oxen will have near a ton to draw as it is, and we'll not add to the weight with wheels hub-deep in mud."

And they had to leave soon, certainly before the month was out, or they would never make the long journey while the weather was good for traveling, claim their land, and establish some kind of shelter before another winter set in.

What to take? What to leave? The questions sounded through the house during the day and often into the night, persistent as the ticking of the clock that stood on the mantel.

"John, I *want* to take this."

"But, Annah, you can't!"

"John, do you have to take that?"

"Annah, I must."

"Pa, here's old Jack's saddle."

"No room, Mark. Put it back in the barn."

"But, Pa, what will we do when we have a horse again?"

"We'll trade with the Indians, son. We'll get a saddle, somehow, out there."

Carolina watched and listened and held Lyddy close to her, feeling safe in her father's promise that she and her doll would not be parted.

In the dooryard was a pile of necessary equipment that John Putnam had assembled and that he was gradually stowing into the wagon — ax, spade, and hoe; hammer, nails, and building tools; a few wide pine boards and four stools; lengths of rope and chains, whip thongs; the grindstone — heavy as that was it was essential, for tools were of little use without sharp edges. Swinging from the rear axle was a leather bucket filled half with tar, half with tallow, and as necessary for wheels and king-bolt each night as was grazing for the oxen.

Near the door rock, Annah Putnam had gathered the equipment for which she was responsible. Piece by piece it would be stowed away in the wagon, some in the compartments beneath the floor, some handy for use on the journey: scissors, needles, thread, and lengths of cotton cloth; beeswax and tallow candles; skillet, kettle, iron pot and bake oven; three wooden buckets — one with lard, one with soap, and the third empty for water; plates, mugs, spoons, knives and forks; washbowl, earthenware jug, and tin lantern; herbs and liniment for doctoring. And the food — a barrel of flour and a small amount of yeast, dried beans and peas, salt, sugar, and vinegar. From the wagon hoops hung a side of smoked beef, two slabs of bacon, and apples dried last October. Because they would take tea instead of coffee beans, the coffee mill could be left behind and there would be one less item of weight. Bedding and clothes would be used for padding.

John looked at the pile, knowing there was nothing there but what had to be taken.

"And the chair, John, it can go?"

"Yes, we'll take it, one slat-back chair."

"And Bossie? Can't we tie her to the back of the wagon? She could keep up with the oxen."

John shook his head. "She's too old, Annah. She'll stay with the farm, as will the chickens. If we can't buy fresh milk and butter now and again along the way, we'll go without."

A dozen times a day as Annah went through the kitchen, she

lifted her eyes to the clock on the mantel. "Wait, old friend" — she smiled at it — "you'll not be left behind. We'll stow you away at the last. We need your reminders until then."

Mark, with his compass safe in his pocket, would gladly have parted with anything else, even his copper-toed boots that he wore only on Sundays and in the winter, as long as his fish pole, the three hooks, and the tin box for bait went along; but of these there was no question. Mark's pole was as necessary for the family as was John Putnam's gun. The only fresh food they would have along the way would be fish from the rivers they crossed and game from the woods that bordered the road. The pole was latched to the ribs that held the canvas in place; the hooks were tucked away in the tin box and stowed in the opening under the wagon seat where the gunpowder was stored, the bowie knife, the medicinal supplies, and the tinder-box. That was the safest place of all the space in the wagon, the driest, and the most accessible. There the Bible was laid, wrapped in a soft woolen shawl.

Big as the book was, and heavy, John Putnam would no more have left it behind than he would his grindstone. "We'll have need to keep an edge to our minds," he said, "and we'll do it best with the Bible."

Carolina brought to the door rock the wooden box that contained Lydia-Lou's clothes and the bed with four small posts her father had made and her mother had covered with a quilt pieced from bits of Carolina's dresses. Beside these she set

Lyddy in her cherry-wood chair. Carolina looked at the box and the bed and the chair and tried to decide which one to take.

"Lyddy," she said, "would you like to have along all your dresses so you can have something different to wear as you do here each day of the week? Or would you like to have some of them?"

The doll returned her china gaze, and Carolina was satisfied.

"That's just what I thought, Lyddy; only, I didn't want to say it first. 'There' won't be like 'here,' so why should you do 'there' what you do 'here'? I'll put on your brown linsey-woolsey, same as mine, and under it I'll put your blue calico, and under it I'll put your pink gingham. That's what Mama's going to do with me, Lyddy, and we'll wear our clothes till we wear them out."

After she had finished dressing Lyddy, she tied a square of blue calico around her neck for a kerchief and took a piece of blue ribbon from the box to use as a sash; then she stood Lyddy against her little chair. "And now, my dear, is it your bed or your chair that you will take along? For both it cannot be, you know."

She leaned close to catch the whisper of a preference.

"I think you've made a very good decision, Lyddy. None of us will be sleeping in beds for a long time, and you wouldn't want to be different. Wait for me, right where you are, Lyddy, while I put away the things we won't be wanting any more."

Box under one arm, bed under the other, Carolina went into the house to the deep closet that opened off the sleeping room. There was a low shelf at one end, and on it she placed the box with Lyddy's remaining clothes and the bed with its four small posts. She stood quietly for a moment, hoping that someday another little girl might find them both and love them as she had.

The feeling of empty space around her was a curious one. Usually the closet was so filled with clothes and quilts and feather pillows that she had to squeeze her way past them all to the shelf at the end. Now there was no need to squeeze past anything, and it was like this throughout the house. One room after another was empty, the way the wagon had been two short weeks ago. Much still remained on shelves and in cupboards. Much had been given to friends and neighbors, and more would be. The big bed with its small trundle stood waiting for others to use, as did the kitchen table, the settle, and all but one slat-back chair.

"The sun tonight speaks well for the morrow," John Putnam said as he returned to the house from his evening chores. "We'll be on our way soon after sunup."

Only the house that had seen years of living could have said what were the thoughts of the four who slept under its roof for the last time, but creaking floor boards keep their secrets.

Sometime during the night rain drummed on the roof, but long before dawn it had ceased. When John Putnam came from the barn with the morning's milk, his eyes met the rim of the rising sun. The day was sparkling around him. There was bird-song in the trees. The fields were showing first faint touches of green. Something tugged at his heart as the heavy pail tugged at his arm. He looked before him — but not at the rounded hills to the east or across the greening fields, not at the small white house lying snug to the ground with a curl of smoke rising from its chimney. No, just then he did not dare look at any of the familiar things. Instead his eyes turned toward the great wagon with its white canvas top that stood in the door-yard, loaded and waiting; then toward the oxen tethered nearby, stolidly munching the hay he had tossed to them earlier.

"In an hour we'll be on our way," he said aloud to the morning.

The Putnam family had a breakfast that they would long remember — milk sweet and warm, and when they would taste such again they did not know; eggs found by Mark in the mow, and fresh as the day; bread crumbling with newness, a loaf from the batch of six Annah had made yesterday and saved out when she stowed the other five in the food box in the wagon. They bowed their heads as they sat at the kitchen table.

"God blessed our coming into this house fifteen years ago," John Putnam said, and it was hard to tell whether he was praying or making a last entry in some invisible book. "He blessed us with Mark, and later on with Carolina. Now may He bless our going out as we seek another land and work for our hands. And may He bless the family that will be sitting around this table by nightfall."

They said "Amen," for it was a prayer, and one in which each had a part.

After breakfast Carolina helped her mother wash their few dishes and put them away for other hands to find and use. She swept the floor and brushed cold ashes over the warm embers on the hearth. Mark had gone with his father to yoke the oxen and back them up to the wagon tongue.

"Time to go," John Putnam called.

Carolina ran out to the wagon with Lyddy under one arm and the little cherry-wood chair under the other.

"Up front with you, daughter, and I'll lift you onto the seat."

She stood beside him, waiting to be lifted.

He looked down at her. "*Both* arms full? That's not the way to travel; one hand must always be free. You'll have to choose, Carolina."

"Papa, you said I could take Lyddy's cherry-wood chair! Can't you find a place for it in the wagon?"

He shook his head. "I'm sorry, Carolina. When I said that, it seemed as if there would be plenty of room, but look for yourself! Where would it go and not be in the way?"

"I'll hold it on my lap."

He shook his head. "Choose, Carolina."

She stood still for a moment, then turned and set Lyddy down to lean against a lilac whose buds had begun to swell in the April sun. She went into the house, into the empty closet, and placed the chair beside the box of clothes and the little four-posted bed. As she ran back through the kitchen, she saw her mother reaching up to the mantel for the clock.

Carolina picked up Lyddy and stood by her father, who hoisted her up and set her down on the wagon seat. She cradled Lyddy in her arms and smiled into the serene china face. "It's all right, Lyddy," she whispered; "you'll always have my arms to rest in when you get a mite tired."

Annah Putnam stood beside the wagon, waiting for her husband to give her a hoist up to the seat. In her arms she held the clock, carefully, for it was still ticking, though she knew she could not keep it running during the journey. Once it ran down, she would not wind it again until it was set up in their new home; sod house or cabin, it could yet be the pulsing heart of their days.

"You need free hands, Annah. There'll often be times when you'll have to take my place."

"Isn't there room inside, John, just for this one more piece?"

"Annah, I'm sorry, but you know as well as I about the room in the wagon and the weight for the oxen." He looked at her tenderly. "Dear Annah, it's hard to have to part with our possessions, but we're not householders any longer; we're pioneers and we have a long, long journey to make."

Annah caught her breath quickly and turned the clock to look at its face. Carolina had been watching her parents, but she gazed away and stared at Mark, who was leaning against the well house, whittling a stick and looking, just then, as if he would not mind waiting a long time. Carolina heard her mother's voice.

"Old friend," she was saying, "you've ticked away all the years we've lived in this house, but it's other folk you'll tick for now, not us."

"Thank you, Annah."

"It's right, John. I know it's right. It would be so much harder later on." She went back to the house.

When she returned to the wagon empty-handed, Carolina looked toward her in time to see her father slip his hand under her mother's arm to lift her up to the seat. Then quickly he closed his arm around her and held her to him, kissing her as if to seal her sacrifice with his love.

Once Annah Putnam was up on the wagon seat, Carolina snuggled close, feeling heart-sorry for her. "Haven't you anything of your own, the way I have Lyddy?" she whispered.

Annah's eyes were on her husband and her son as they moved to take their places, one on the left, one on the right, of the oxen. "Oh, yes," she said, and suddenly her voice sounded as bright as the morning, "the pots and pans in the wagon, the needles and thread —"

"And us?"

"Yes, Carolina, all of you. Yes, indeed."

"Gee-up!" John Putnam shouted, cracking his whip high.

"Gee-up!" Mark echoed, slapping his hand on the rump of the ox near him.

The oxen strained forward. The wagon jolted and came to a standstill.

Three times the whip cracked in the air. Three times the voices commanded and coaxed. At last, with a shuddering groan and a creaking of wheels, the wagon lurched forward. Inside, under the canvas top, there was a chattering muttera-tion, as if all the items so carefully stowed away were talking together. The wagon moved, out of the dooryard and onto the road.

There were places where the road was still soft, and at times the wheels went deep, but not axle-deep. Once the oxen got the feel of their load, they moved steadily on. Old Jack lifted his head in the pasture and trotted clumsily across the field, whin-nying shrilly. Bossie looked up from her grazing, and mooed. The chickens pecked in the barnyard, and in the empty house the clock on the mantel ticked away in the silence.

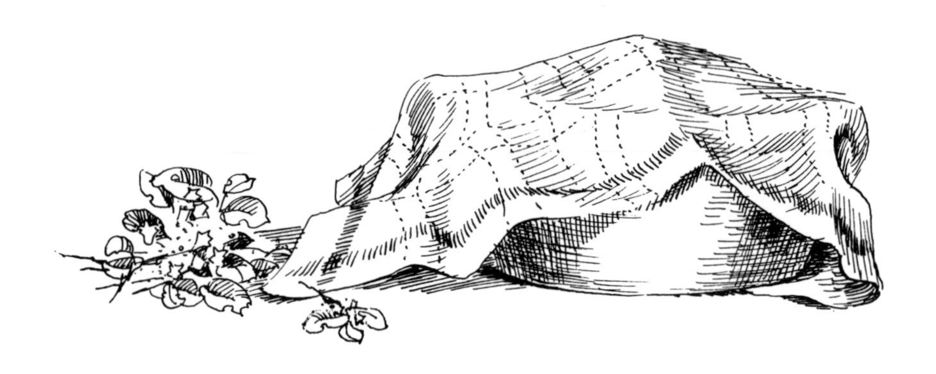

Chapter three

IT WAS SLOW, going down the long hill to the village with one wheel chained to hold the wagon back. The movements of the oxen were jerky. But once the level road was reached and the wheel was unchained, the oxen adjusted themselves to the weight of the load and bent their strength to it, drawing the wagon evenly. As the Putnam family moved through the village, people came to their doorways to wave, to wish them a good journey and a safe settling at the end.

"Write us when you get located!"

"Let us know if it all is as good as it sounds!"

"Perhaps we'll meet you someday west of the Mississippi!"

No one said "Come back" or "See you soon" or any of the friendly words that were often said at leave-taking, for they knew that once a family started toward the western territory there was no coming back. When a man sold house and land and a woman parted with all but a few of her possessions, their life had its stake in the future, no matter what that future might be.

The hands that waved farewell were empty, for the villagers were well aware that a settler's wagon had all that it could carry, and often more than it should. Even a basket of eggs would find no room. Only at the small white house near the church did a woman leave her doorway and come toward the wagon. In her hands was an earthenware dish covered with a cloth.

"It's a meat pie, warm from the oven," the parson's wife said as she walked along beside John Putnam and handed it up to Annah while the oxen maintained their steady pace. "It will taste good when you rest at nooning. It will taste like home."

Close to the woman ran a little girl. In her hands was a small bunch of Mayflowers. "I found them in the woods this morning. They're the first, the very first," she said as she offered them to John Putnam, who handed them up to Carolina.

Carolina pressed the flowers to her nose, and by the time she took them away the two had ceased walking along beside the wagon and were standing in the road, waving.

"Goodbye!"

"Goodbye, goodbye."

Even the clock in the steeple said it seven times: "God be with you, God be with you —"

Now the village was left behind as up the long incline to the westward the Putnam family went. The road was firm, and the oxen drew the wagon well. At the crest of the hill John Putnam called a rest. The oxen were breathing hard, and their flanks were steaming. The sun shone on the little white village in the valley, on the houses where people were going about their chores, on the cattle and sheep in the pastures, on a man plowing his field.

Gazing back, down the long hill up which they had come, Carolina thought how dear and sheltered the village looked, as if God had cupped it in the palm of His hand.

"Stretch your legs, Carolina," John Putnam said as he reached up for his daughter and set her on the ground to stand beside him.

There was a spring near the road, and they all drank from it; then John Putnam filled the leather bucket that hung on the wagon's rear axletree and offered water to the oxen so they might allay their thirst. "At nooning they can drink their fill," he said, "but now, in the midst of work, a little will satisfy them."

After Carolina took some moss from near the spring to wrap around the Mayflowers, she sat with her back against a tree and talked to Lyddy while her father sprawled on the ground nearby. Mark and Annah Putnam walked up the road a few rods from the wagon, first on one side and then the other, and all the time Annah kept her eyes down as if she were looking for a lost thimble in the grass.

"What are you searching for?" her husband called.

"Might be some dandy-lions that we could eat, or some poke-weed shoots to have for a sallet."

"Not here, not now, Annah; too early, too high. Wait till we get into York State and you'll find all you can use. Spring comes quicker there."

In another quarter of an hour John Putnam called to his family. He helped Annah onto the seat and hoisted Carolina up beside her; then he told Mark to climb into the back of the wagon. Mark settled down among the bedding, resting against his will but at his father's bidding. In the afternoon he would walk beside the oxen while his father rested. There was a short level stretch, then a wheel was chained again and the oxen plodded down another hill. This was the hill beyond which the sun had always set, and Carolina had once thought of it as the rim of the world.

At midday they had reached a grassy place by a shallow stream, and there they spent the next two hours. The oxen grazed and drank and comforted their hoofs by standing in soft mud. The Putnam family was ready for rest and food, too. Dinner was made of the dish the parson's wife had given them when it was warm from her oven and which had been kept somewhat warm by the sun. It was a hearty meat stew with many potatoes, and they ate until the dish was empty and they could hold no more; then Annah washed it in the stream and dried it in the breeze.

"Maybe we'll meet someone who'll be going back the

way we've just come and who'll return it for us," she said.

Before the afternoon was half over, they did meet a peddler on his way east. He gladly took the dish and the cloth that was folded in it, stowed it away in his high-wheeled cart among his wares, and promised to leave it at the parsonage before nightfall. He gave them a fair description of the road ahead and told John Putnam of a likely place where they might spend the night. Then, with a smile, a cheery wish, and a flip of the reins over the back of his horse, he was down the road and soon out of sight. In a matter of minutes he covered a space it had taken them an hour to traverse.

Mark sighed as he watched the peddler. "Pa, why aren't we going west with a team of horses? Oxen are so slow."

"Slow they are, son, but they'll get us there and without too great cost. Horses require different food. We could no more spare room in the wagon to carry oats than we could afford to buy them along the way. We'll have to be patient, the way the oxen are, and they'll work as hard for us when we get to our land as they do on the journey."

"But the peddler —"

"Oh, he'll do more than twice the miles we will in a day, but that's his life. We're settlers, and if we do a hundred miles westward in a week, with a good place to rest each night, we'll be doing well. Take over, Mark, while I ride in the wagon for a while."

Mark grasped his father's whip in his hand and cracked it

high in the air. Its meaning was clear to the oxen, and they moved forward. "Giddap, there!" Mark shouted as he fell into step beside them.

The wagon creaked on into and through the afternoon.

The sun was setting when John Putnam called to the team, "Gee-over. Gee! I tell you."

The oxen drew the wagon off the road to the right and toward a clump of birches that bordered a river. When "Whoa!" was shouted, they came to a standstill and stood waiting.

John Putnam and Mark tethered the oxen near the water so they could drink and graze and cool their feet as they wished; then they built a fire near the wagon, got all in readiness for the evening meal, and gathered sufficient wood to last through the night. The iron kettle was taken from the wagon, swung over the fire, and Annah Putnam was soon as busy with it as she would have been in her kitchen at home. After they had eaten, a small tent was set up between the wagon and the fire where the men of the family would sleep. Bedding was arranged and sorted out so there would be warmth and comfort within the tent, as well as within the wagon for the women of the family, for though the day had been warm the cool of evening was making itself felt.

Carolina's eyes had begun to close almost before the meal was over, and when beds were arranged her father took her up in his arms and placed her in her corner in the wagon. She held Lyddy close to her and smiled sleepily as she felt the snug comfort of quilts being tucked around her.

"Are we almost there?" she whispered.

"We've gone twenty miles, little daughter. That's a long day's journey for the oxen."

He kissed her and went out to join the others, who were sitting by the bright coals of the fire.

"Twenty miles!" Carolina said to Lyddy; then she made a song of it. The words were her own, but the music that went with them came from the night around her — the gentle swish of the river as it moved along through the darkness, the slow munching of the oxen and an occasional stamp of a hoof, the murmur of voices from the three who sat by the fire, and the distant *clip-clop* of a horse and rider on the road. They were all good and friendly sounds. Carolina felt as safe in the wagon as she knew that Lyddy felt safe in her arms.

"Twenty miles, Lydia-Lou, from our old home to our new," she crooned softly. "Twenty miles, did you hear Papa say? And we'll do the same when tomorrow's today."

Long before daybreak John Putnam was astir, and soon afterward Annah resumed her work preparing the early-morning meal, serving it, then washing their few dishes, tidying up and dousing the fire while the men yoked the oxen to the wagon and made ready for the journey. Soon after sunup they were on their way.

This was the pattern of the days as the wagon creaked its

slow way up and down the hills of New England, then along the more level and traveled route of York State. Sometimes John Putnam drove the oxen, sometimes Mark, and for an hour or two each day Carolina trotted beside her mother when Annah took over their charge. Most of the time Carolina sat in the wagon and played with Lyddy, or perched herself on the wooden seat to watch the countryside through which they were passing.

In New Hampshire and Vermont, men had been plowing their fields; in New York they were planting; in Ohio they were hoeing and cultivating their crops; in Indiana they were haying. Six days a week the Putnams spent on the road, but the seventh they spent in a sheltered and watered place beside the road. Not all wagon families did so, but John Putnam was firm in his feeling that one day belonged to the Lord, and was for rest. The Bible was taken out from the wagon box, and reading it became a center for their day. When Monday morning dawned they were all, including the oxen, refreshed and eager for the miles ahead.

There were occasional rainy days that enforced rest. During them the family sat in the wagon with canvas drawn tight for protection, read or wrote a letter, mended clothes or equipment, and waited out the weather. There were days when they came to a halt early in the afternoon because the countryside offered the chance to restock their food supplies. Mark went to a nearby river or lake with his pole and came back with a string of fish for their dinner. John Putnam took his gun to the woods and came back with game. Annah, with time at hand, set up the tin oven by the fire and did a week's baking.

These were days that Carolina relished. When her father returned from hunting and put his gun away in the wagon, he would take her into the woods with him for a time together. She was getting too big to ride on his shoulders now, and she was proud of the fact that she could match her stride to his. They would go to a secret place that he had discovered earlier, often near a spring, and there they would sit quietly, and wait.

"There's no telling what we may see, Carolina, if we sit still for a bit."

"Might it be a bear?" She shivered, and held her father's hand tighter, glad just then that she had left Lyddy in the safety of the wagon.

"Not a bear in these parts, nor a catamount. It could be a raccoon, coming to wash his food in the spring. It could be a bird with scarlet feathers and a song that's sweet and wild and like nothing you've ever heard before."

"But if it were a bear?"

"We'd sit still, Carolina, and he'd go about the business that brought him here. He'd pay us no mind at all."

After such a time, Carolina always had a great deal to tell Lyddy about when she got back to the wagon.

There were days, especially as the heat of the summer increased, when John Putnam turned the oxen into the dooryard of a farm, hailed the farmer, and offered to hire himself and Mark for a few hours' labor. "And in return, I'd like my beasts to have rest in your pasture. I'd like fresh food for my family — milk, eggs, and some green things you may have ripening."

The offer was never refused, and the payment was always generous.

While the men were working in the fields, or helping to build a barn or turning their hands to whatever needed doing, Annah would help the farmer's wife with churning or washing or quilting, or wherever the household could use an extra pair of hands. Carolina played with the children, jumping in their haymow, climbing their apple trees. Lydia-Lou would be set up among their dolls and coaxed to tell of her life as the other dolls told of theirs.

Once, at the eastern edge of Illinois, they stayed three whole days at a farm. John Putnam and Mark helped the farmer get all his hay in while the weather held, and Annah helped in the house with a new baby. Carolina played with two little boys, as alike as two kernels on an ear of corn. She slept in a trundle bed and ate from dishes at a table, and she liked living such a life again. On the fourth morning, when the oxen were brought in from the field and yoked to the wagon, Carolina did not want to leave.

"Can't we stay here, Papa?"

"For another day and night?"

"No, for always."

John Putnam shook his head. "This isn't our land, Carolina. Ours is ahead, waiting for us."

"Where?"

"Across the Mississippi, and then a little farther. You'll find friends there, as you've found them along the way. They may be different, as everything will be different, but a pioneer must put up with what he finds."

Fiercely Carolina clasped Lyddy to her. "I don't care about any friends; I've got my Lydia-Lou."

Annah Putnam came from the house toward the wagon. She held in her hand a piece of something blue that fluttered in the hot July breeze. The farm wife, her baby in her arms, stood in the doorway. Close to her were the two little boys who stared at Carolina, now that she was leaving them, as if she were the stranger she had been when she arrived.

"Goodbye! Good journeying! Thank you."

"Goodbye! Keep well, and thank you kindly."

Friendly words filled the air, but no one said "Come back and see us again sometime," as no one had said that when the Putnams left New Hampshire. A pioneer family knew only one road: the road ahead, the road that led into the West. Not until the oxen pulled away from the dooryard and the wagon was rolling over the road again did Annah Putnam show her daughter the piece of blue cloth she had been holding ever since she came from the house.

"It's a new dress for Lyddy," she said, as she smoothed it across her lap. "Seems to me she needs one. She'll be coming to her new home before many days."

Carolina clapped her hands together at the sight of the pretty dress. It had a neat little bodice with a tiny button at the throat, a series of tucks down the skirt, and a scarlet sash.

"I was making a dress for the baby. There was a bit of cloth left over, and I fashioned this for Lydia-Lou."

"Mama, Mama —" Carolina breathed, as delight took her words away. Then she climbed back into the wagon and settled herself amidst the bedding.

Carolina took off Lyddy's brown dress, realizing as she did so how travel-worn it was. Over the china head with its smooth black hair she slipped the new blue dress and tied the scarlet sash with a tidy bow. It was handsome, Carolina thought; oh, it was handsome indeed; but she knew that she would not permit Lyddy to wear it all the time, just sometimes. It must be kept fresh for Lyddy to wear when they got to their new home.

"Across the big river," she whispered to Lyddy.

The days were long and very hot. The country was flat. The roads were hard and dry, often dusty. Sometimes the oxen were able to travel close to thirty miles in a single day, but John Putnam did not urge them beyond their natural power. They would be needed for work once the new land was reached, and he wanted to keep them fit. The wagonload was still almost as heavy, for though food was continually consumed their stores were frequently replenished. At one time the villages had been no more than a day's journey apart; now they were three days or more, and often neither homestead nor cabin was passed from sunup to sundown.

John Putnam was glad that they had not yet been forced to lighten their load for the sake of the oxen. More than one wagon family had been obliged to jettison some of its belongings, as occasional objects along the way bore witness. Once they passed a rocking chair, rocking in the prairie wind as if an invisible person were sitting in it. Once it was a churn and, not a half-mile farther on, an iron cooking pot. One day they saw standing, alone and like a sentinel, a tall grandfather clock. It was ticking away the time in the emptiness of space.

"Oh," Annah exclaimed at the sight, "how could they part with such an old family friend!"

"Oxen getting spent, load had to be lightened," John Putnam said.

Annah caught her breath. "I couldn't have left our clock along the road."

"You might have had to."

"It's better where it is, with somebody to wind it and dust it and heed it, though I don't know that somebody."

Toward evening of the same day they passed a little cradle left by the road. It was too small for any baby.

"Seems as if it would have been mighty sad if Carolina had had to leave Lyddy's cherry-wood chair or her four-posted bed along the way."

"Oh, John, you made those for her yourself! I remember the weeks you took in carving the spindles — in polishing —"

"Best not to remember," he said quietly. "Besides, arms were meant for cradling. Carolina's been happy with Lyddy in her arms."

The next day they reached the Mississippi. Somewhere on the other side, perhaps only a few weeks distant, lay their land. Rain, long needed, swept down over the dry countryside. The oxen relished its coolness on yoke-weary shoulders. Inside the wagon, the family drew the puckering strings tight against the wet.

"When it clears," John Putnam announced, "the flatboat will get us across. Until then, we're blest to have a canvas roof to keep us dry."

Chapter four

ONCE THEY were on the west side of the Mississippi, they turned in a slightly more northerly direction and followed a well-traveled route that led to the crossing of the Missouri River. It was more than a week's journey, more than a hundred miles, and much of the way led through Indian country. The road was not marked, as earlier roads had been, but it could not be missed. Ruts had been worn deep by the passing of heavy wagons, and the prairie grass had been flattened so that a natural trail led through it.

The next river, and the last for them of any size, was the Kansas. A ferry was there, maintained by Indians, and there the Putnams had a first experience in trading. When the wagon started on its way again, it had lost some yards of cotton cloth, a few small tools, and gained by buckskin jackets and moccasins for them all.

An ancient squaw, with a face like a dried apple, approached the wagon as it was moving and held up a basket of blueberries. She gestured to Anna's neckerchief.

Annah laughed as she untied it and handed it to the woman. "We'll eat fresh fruit tonight, and I can do well enough without this."

"Pioneer folk must be willing to share," John Putnam added as he cracked his whip in the air and the oxen drew the wagon forward.

Carolina peeped out from behind the canvas opening, glad that she had hid Lyddy under the bedding. Who could ever know what an Indian might take a fancy to!

It was not until they were well away from the ferry that Mark dared to reach into his pocket and close his fingers around his compass. "I wouldn't want to trade this for all the buckskin jackets and berries in the Nebraska Territory," he said to his father as he walked along beside him.

"Hope you'll never have to, son, but a traveler in Indian land often has to trade his way."

Mark returned the compass to safety in his pocket.

"Two weeks to the Platte River," John Putnam told his family. "There's a supply post at the crossing, and it's there we'll be given our claim."

Two weeks: Annah saw herself unpacking the wagon and setting up a home again.

As they moved slowly along the rutted way through a sea of waving blue-stemmed prairie grass, they often came upon reminders of those who had gone before them. Sometimes a wagon family left a note beside the trail. As there were no trees to nail it to, and no stones to hold it down, it would be tucked into a mound of earth with only a portion visible. It might tell where water was, or where a wagon encampment would be made, or whether the Indians were friendly. John Putnam, reading it, would be informed or alerted, and before tucking it back into the earth for the next family to read he would add a line or two by way of prairie conversation.

Plodding slowly on under the hot August sun, they were made to realize that the easy comfort and accepted safety of their journey were now behind them. This was rugged land, perhaps even hostile. It was dry land. The streams and water holes were few, and they had to be sure of reaching one by day's end. Sometimes they could travel ten miles only, for beyond that there was no water for thirty miles. In such country it was needful to start out each morning with every vessel that could hold water filled to its capacity. And, in such country, it was not easy to find fuel for their fire at night. Small sticks of sagebrush and buffalo chips often had to do for burning, and even these were not always easily found.

There were days when they saw nothing but herds of buffalo roaming in the distance, and there were other days when chance meetings gave them much to talk about. People coming toward them were their means of information, as were the notes left in the earth. More than one trapper on his way back to the

trading post at Independence, Missouri, told them of what the land ahead held.

One day an Indian riding across the prairie approached them. He held his right hand across his heart, and John Putnam understood it as a gesture of friendship and responded by placing his own right hand across his heart. From the Indian, not with words but through signs, they learned where sweet water could be found.

The next day a pioneer, who had already staked his claim and built his cabin, met them. He was on his way back to Independence, Missouri, to collect his family. He drove two spans of mules, and his near-empty wagon covered distance easily. He spent a night with the Putnams, sharing their food and his information. He drew a map of the country ahead and gave valuable suggestions about the land. When he went on his way, John Putnam felt heartened by all that he had learned. "That's a man we're like to see again," he said.

Two days later there was an encounter of another kind.

Coming across the prairie toward them was a wagon; its white top seen through the tall grass, then not seen as the land dipped and rose again, looked like a lonely sail on a wide green sea.

"Slow traveling means a heavy load," John Putnam commented.

It was not until midafternoon that the wagon came near enough for them to see a woman walking barefoot beside her oxen, and three small children sitting on the seat.

"Where's your man?" John Putnam asked, as the wagons met and came to a halt.

"Killed by the Indians. I'm taking the young ones home, though we've no home left to go to. A woman can't pioneer without a man when her young ones are as small as mine."

"Rest yourselves for a spell," John Putnam said.

The children clung to each other on the wagon seat while

the woman leaned against one of her oxen and told her story, a brief and bitter story.

A party of Indians had surrounded their wagon and demanded some of its goods. "They wanted our sugar, at least as near as we could tell what it was they wanted with their gibberish and their gestures, but my man said No. He told them he hadn't toted fifty pounds of sugar all the way from Connecticut to give to those who had no need for it. He reached for his gun, and what did he get but an arrow in his heart!"

Annah murmured words of compassion, and John asked the woman if she would not wheel around and go on again with them; but she was determined to return east.

"You'll stop long enough to have a meal with us," the Putnams urged.

The woman shook her head. "Get along there," she called to her oxen, and the wagon moved slowly forward.

They watched her go until she had almost disappeared into the distance from which they had come.

"That sugar might have given them clear passage," John Putnam said; then he called to Mark and Carolina to come out of the wagon and walk beside the oxen while he climbed up to the seat to sit beside his wife. Grimly he stared before him as they went on their way.

North of west their course had lain ever since they had crossed the last river, and now the afternoon sun, instead of blinding them as it had for so much of their journey, cast

long shadows over the prairie grass to their right. Only the shapes of the oxen and the wagon were distinct in the shadows; all else had been swallowed up in their darkness.

Annah, more than once, had had to still the fear that rose in her heart like an incoming tide; this time she could not hold it back. Never had the prairie seemed so vast, the sun so hot, the day so filled with possible evil. She spoke her fear to her husband, but softly. What she had to say, just then, was for his ears alone.

"I don't like what's ahead."

"It's the hardest part of the journey, Annah, but we're less than a week now to our claim. Another month and you'll have a roof of sorts over your head, and some kind of hearth."

"But, John, if we meet with an unfriendly Indian, *what will you do?"*

"Say 'Indian,' Annah. This is Pawnee country, and they have long been friendly to settlers."

"How will they know that we are friendly?"

"My open hands held out to them will show that I hold no weapon."

"But—but, John, if they want something of us, how are we to know what it is they want?"

"There are ways of understanding, and we've got enough to share."

His words did not quell her fears entirely, but Annah knew there was no going back for any of them, whatever the days ahead might hold.

That night, when the oxen were unyoked and tethered, when the fire had been made and their meal cooked and eaten and they sat near it for a time of quiet before they went to their sleep, Annah had no eyes for the beauty of the star-decked sky above them and no ears for the song of the wind in the prairie grass around them. From the hills ahead of them, hills through which they would soon be passing, Indian fires were flaring. Annah shivered at the sight and told the children to sleep under cover in the wagon. Later, when she tucked Carolina into the bedding and smoothed a blanket over Mark, she called out to her husband from the wagon.

"Aren't you coming in to rest, John?"

"Not yet awhile," he said, as he sat by the fire.

Carolina was crooning to Lyddy. "There's nothing to fear, my Lydia-Lou; Mama's got me and I've got you. Mark's got Papa and he's got—" She lifted her head from the bedding and looked up at her mother. "Who's Papa got to keep him from being afraid?"

Annah did not answer. She glanced out again at the man by the fire. The light from the coals showed his lean body bent slightly forward, his hands held out to the warmth. Beyond him was the black vastness of the prairie and the starry sky. He looked lonely, as that first man in Eden must have looked, and yet, as that first man also must have known, she knew that he was not alone. Annah compelled her voice to be steady as she answered her daughter.

"He's got God, Carolina. Now, turn over and go to sleep. And you, too, Mark; morning will be upon us all too soon, and you both know what morning means. And I don't want either one of you to leave the wagon without telling me."

"Why, Ma?"

"Because I say so, that's why."

Carolina slid down into the bedding and held Lyddy to her. It seemed odd to want to draw the covers close when it was such a hot night.

Once she lifted her head and peeked out from the covers. Her mother was near, near enough to touch, but she was on her knees beside her quilt, and Carolina knew what that meant. The night seemed very dark and still. It would be a long time till morning. Carolina began to wonder if morning would ever come, or if the Indians would descend on their wagon during the night and—she shuddered, and closed her eyes tight. She did not want to remember some of the stories that were told when wagon folk met. She did not want to think of the lone woman trudging back east and her three small children. Nor would she. When her father had first begun to talk about moving west, he had said they would all have to be brave. She did not want to lose heart now when they were within a week of their goal. She opened her eyes, but it was too dark to see how far the wide flat land stretched in every direction. At home — no, she must not say that now; home lay ahead. Back east, the sky had always seemed so near and the hills had enfolded them.

"Dear God," she whispered into the stillness, "keep our journey safe."

A burst of song from a prairie lark broke out of the sky, and light began to flow over the land. John Putnam stirred the fire with the toe of his boot, then stood up, reached out his arms, and looked around him. All was still in the wagon. The oxen were lying quietly, front legs folded under powerful chests, dew glistening on their brown coats. He looked west where a herd of antelope was fleeting across the prairie. Beyond the low rise of the hills was the land he would claim as his — rich black bottom land with river water running through it and timbered on the north. A hundred acres were waiting for him, his for the working, his and Annah's to have and to hold, to make fruitful and to enjoy. He lifted his arm and saluted the morning; then he raised both arms as if to embrace his land. Leaning down, he took up the water bucket; but before going to the spring he called awakening to his family asleep in the wagon.

In less than an hour they were on their way, for the fresh cool morning hours were the best time of the day for traveling. Twenty miles, and they would be on the banks of a creek where several wagons would have gathered to rest their oxen and secure directions for the last push each family had to make to reach a claim in the broad valley of the Platte River.

Annah and John, in their strength and eagerness, strode beside the oxen, but their pace was longer than that of the animals and they were constantly having to stop and wait for the wagon to come abreast of them. It was good to be alive on such a morning. They had been walking into the future for four months. Now it seemed that the future was at last coming to meet them. Fears felt during the night had shrunk to daylight size, and the family talked together easily and naturally.

Mark and Carolina sat on the wagon seat. Carolina was busy putting Lyddy into her best dress and telling her how she

should behave when they reached the encampment. Mark was busy whittling a willow whistle.

"You're getting Lyddy ready for her homecoming too soon, aren't you?"

"I want her to look nice when we meet the wagon folks tonight. Papa says there may be as many as five wagons at the creek crossing. That means lots of children, and Lyddy will be able to meet some of her own kind and hear their news."

Mark put his whistle up to his lips, pleased at the trickle of sound that came from it.

"That's pretty! What are you aiming to do at the encampment?"

"Catch some fish for our supper, first thing," Mark said. "It could be that folks will get to singing around their fires, and I could make music right along with them."

Carolina lowered her voice. "Mark, is that Indian country ahead — those hills lying low against the sky?"

He nodded.

"Friendly or unfriendly?"

He shrugged his shoulders.

"What would you do if you met an Indian?"

"I would — I would offer him my hand to show him that I wanted to be his friend."

"Wouldn't you be afraid?"

"If I was, way down inside myself, I wouldn't show it."

Mark went back to his whittling, occasionally putting the whistle to his lips and blowing on it. Carolina relayed to Lydia-Lou all her recent information.

"Everything will be all right, Lyddy," she said, "if you just don't act as if you were afraid. Remember that I'm near, and I'll hold you in my arms and that way you'll always be safe. You do understand, don't you?"

Lyddy's smooth china face answered Carolina's question with complete assurance.

"Yes, that's just what I think, Lyddy; but, remember, you're not to go any place without me. Why? Oh, Lyddy, how can you ask such a question? It's because I say it, that's why."

By early afternoon they could see ahead of them the cluster of wagons that had gathered at the creek. Smoke was curling up from their fires. A cheerful hum of voices mingled with an occasional low mooing or sharp neighing that came across the open space. The oxen, sensing water ahead and the finer grass that grew beside it, quickened their plodding. One made a rumbling sound; the other lifted his head and bellowed lustily. It was heard at the encampment, and a din went up from the oxen tethered there. Then the people, made aware of the approach of another wagon, began to wave — a skillet here, a kerchief there, whatever came to hand.

"How many white-tops do you see, Mark?"

"Ten, Pa, or maybe eleven."

"That's what I make it, eleven."

"More than we've ever met up with before!" Annah exclaimed happily.

John Putnam shook his head. "It's too many. There must be something holding them up."

"Perhaps there's quicksand in the creek and they're having to build a bridge —"

"Perhaps they're waiting for a land-office man —"

"Perhaps they're waiting for us —"

One after another they voiced their speculations, but John Putnam did not give utterance to the thought that had come to his mind, the thought that the lone woman going back east had not told all her story. Perhaps her man was killed only after he had killed and the Indians had been provoked.

Within the hour they drew into the encampment, and a mighty welcome was given to them. Pioneering folk, once they met up together at supply post or river crossing, were like members of a family, whether they hailed from New Hampshire or Pennsylvania or Kentucky. They knew the weariness of the miles, the privations endured, the dangers faced, and they shared the lure of the land ahead that was worth anything undergone on the way. A wagon from the East was sure to have news, and the west-bound emigrants, though they had severed their ties, were still heart-hungry for word of "home."

"You came through safe these last two, three days?" a man asked John Putnam.

"Safe as we came through Ohio," he answered, "though we could have done with more water. My oxen are about ready to drink the creek dry."

Mark unyoked the oxen and led them to water. Carolina went into the wagon to help her mother roll up the canvas sides.

"Best make yourself at home for a while as the other wagon folk are doing."

"What are you waiting for?" John Putnam asked.

"An interpreter. There'll be a trapper along, or a scout, one of these days who'll be able to talk with the Indians and clear the way for us."

"But why is there need?" John Putnam asked. Tiredness fell away from him in impatience to cover the few remaining miles that stood between him and his claim.

"There must have been some trouble a few days ago out on the prairie, and the Indians are stirred up. We've got to wait until someone comes along who can talk with them and tell them we're honest settlers, not warfaring men."

"Better bide awhile," another added. "What's a week if it means your life?"

John nodded reluctantly. When he told Annah and the children that they might remain at the encampment for a few days rather than just overnight, each one had a reason for being pleased. Mark promptly got his pole and went off to the creek to fish. Carolina took Lyddy in her arms and approached a group of little girls. Annah sighed with relief.

"It will give me a chance to do some washing," she said, "and I'd like to give the wagon a good cleaning before we get to our land."

John Putnam did not relish the enforced rest. There were not many weeks left before the bleakness of winter would come over the prairie, and he wanted to have a shelter established for his family and one for his animals before that time.

"Bide we will if we must," he said, "but I'd rather we could get on our way in the morning. However, I've got a whining wheel to grease and I'm going to see if there's a blacksmith in this crowd of wagons to have a look at the oxen's hoofs."

Annah went about her duties, smiling to herself as she had not done during the past few days. It was good to hear the sound of human voices again — people talking together, children laughing and shouting, a woman calling to her man, a baby crying to be fed. It was good to be a part of human activities again — women washing the family clothes, putting bedding out to air, bringing long-stored-away brooms into use; men repairing their wagons, mending broken tools, rubbing down their animals.

It was all good after the wind-threaded silence of the prairies.

Chapter five

CAROLINA SOON discovered four little girls her own age among the wagon folk. Each one had a doll, but Lydia-Lou was so superior that when they sat down to play she was chosen to be teacher and school was the game. One doll was made of wood, and Carolina thought how hard it must be to cuddle such a child; one was like Lyddy, with china face and hands and feet; one was made of rags tied at the neck to make a head and loosely tied around the middle; and one was shaped from corn husks. Over them all, Lyddy presided.

Sooner or later, one child after another was called away to render help to her parents. Carolina, seeing the washing her own mother was doing, felt that it was high time for Lyddy's brown traveling dress to be washed. She fetched it from the wagon and went with it to the bank of the creek. Upstream the water looked clearer, and there Carolina found a flat stone to kneel on while she swished the dress in the flowing water, slapped it against a stone as she had seen her mother do, and finally wrung it out and hung it on a little bush. She put twigs in the arms so it would dry shapely, since wagon folk rarely did any ironing.

Lydia-Lou, patiently leaning against a tree, watched the whole procedure.

"Now, what shall we do, Lyddy? Even with all this wind and sun your dress won't be dry for a while. We could just sit here by the creek and tell each other stories, or —" She leaned close to the doll, for whatever Lyddy had to say was a secret.

"Do you really want to go exploring, Lyddy? But you've got your best dress on!" She looked earnestly at the china face.

"Very well, then. I'll take your hand, Lyddy, and we'll just go along the creek a little way, and if the going is rough I'll carry you so you won't harm your pretty dress. Perhaps we'll find Mark fishing. If we do, Lyddy, we'll creep up and sit down beside him without saying a word, because Mark doesn't like talk when he's fishing."

They followed a narrow path. Around them, cottonwoods grew tall, willows bowed to the water, and the murmur of wind in green leaves was like a voice from home, for during the long hot days on the prairie there had been no trees to catch the wind and turn it into sound. It was an enchanted world of lush growth along the creek, and to Carolina, born and bred in green New Hampshire, it was friendly and familiar. It seemed to become more beautiful the farther they went. The trees grew thicker as they arched above her, and the small whispering made by the creek as it slipped over stones assured Carolina that she was never far from the encampment where many people were busily occupied and contentedly resting.

The path came to an end at a thicket of birches. Carolina pushed her way into the thicket; then she caught her breath and stood very still. Beyond the low-hanging branches was a small clearing with moss underfoot for a carpet and delicate shimmering leaves for walls and ceiling.

"Oh, Lyddy, it's like a little green room just big enough for us. Shall we pretend it's ours?"

She set Lyddy down on the moss and leaned her back against a birch whose leaves were as shining as coins, and no bigger. She gazed at Lyddy.

"Do you want to play that it is *your* house and *I* have come to take tea with you? Very well, sit quietly then and fold your hands in your lap. Here's a leaf for a saucer and here's a bit of bark for a cup. Here's a stone the creek must have washed up and left, for it's so clean. We'll say it's our teapot. Here are two more saucers and two more cups, because Mama always says a table should be laid not just for the family but for whoever else might happen along."

Lyddy, hands politely folded, watched what Carolina was doing and made her own conversation.

"Lyddy, dear, how pleased I am that you invited me to take tea with you today, and I have so much news to tell you!" Carolina reached out for a cup and saucer and lifted the cup; then she held it in mid-air.

"What's that, Lyddy? You want me to say a blessing? People don't generally, for tea, you know, but I'd do anything for you because it's such a beautiful day and your house is so fine. Let me think a minute."

She placed the cup and saucer down on the moss and closed her eyes. In the silence within the leafy house, Carolina was aware of the near sound of the creek, and that was all. Not even a breeze stirred their little green room.

Lovely thoughts moved within her as she recalled the long journey that was now behind them, of the pleasant stopping by the creek and the many kindly folk from so many places in the East. She thought of her father and mother and Mark, but especially of Lydia-Lou and all that she meant to her. Then, with quivering excitement, she thought of the new home that was now so near, the home they would all help to build.

Carolina never uttered her thoughts in words, for into the silence a sound other than that of running water was making itself heard, a soft low sound as of something on its way through the bushes. A dried leaf crackled, a dead branch snapped, then the sound ceased; but after a brief moment it could be heard again. Carolina's eyes were still shut tight. She knew that she would have to open them, but she did not want to. Lyddy was sitting on the other side of the mossy tea table and Carolina wanted to reach out and grasp her, then hold her close. But she must make no hasty move; of that she was sure. Whatever animal it was that was creeping toward her would not harm her if she remained quite still. Her father had told her that ever since she was a little girl when they had gone into the woods together.

"Don't be afraid, Carolina, and stay very still," she could hear her father say. If he were only near now she would ask him, "But how can I not be afraid when I *am* afraid?"

The sound was growing nearer. Was it a wolf? Or a bear? If it came up and sniffed her all over, could she remain still? She thought that perhaps she could if she had Lyddy in her arms. She opened her eyes and looked across the tea table with its leaf saucers and bark cups and stone teapot.

In a low voice, so low that only Lyddy could hear, for it was scarcely more than her heart speaking, Carolina said: "Don't be afraid, Lyddy. I'm here. I'll take care of you. We're safe because we're together." She reached out slowly, put one hand on Lyddy and drew her to her; then she cradled Lyddy in her arms, covering Lyddy's face so she would not see the fearsome thing whatever it might be.

Carolina felt brave now, more able to remain still until the noisemaker came into the clearing, satisfied its curiosity about her, and went away again.

She stared ahead of her in the direction of the sound, curious herself, and wondering.

Then the branches of a birch were pushed aside and toward the clearing came — not a wolf, not a bear — but a small Indian girl. She crawled through the bushes, under the low-hanging branches, and all the time one hand held something close to her lean body in its fringed buckskin tunic. It was not until she squatted down in the very place where Lyddy had been sitting that Carolina saw what she had been holding so carefully close.

It was a doll, as different from Carolina's doll as Carolina was from the Indian girl. The visitor held her doll forward as if to show it to Carolina; then she cradled it in her arms and rocked it as Carolina had been doing with Lyddy.

Carolina was so relieved that she smiled and then, when she found her tongue, said what she had heard her mother say time and again when a guest arrived unexpectedly, "You're welcome to our home. Come in and bide a while with us."

The Indian girl stared at Carolina, then smiled. Her teeth were very white in her swarthy face, and her black eyes glistened. She said something that to Carolina was meaningless, but after she spoke she laid her doll across her knees and opened both hands, holding them palms up toward Carolina. The gesture was not meaningless, and Carolina replied with a similar one. Then the Indian girl put her left hand to her heart and crossed it with her right. Carolina did the same. A moment later the dolls were repeating the gestures.

The Indian girl pointed to the leaves and bark on the moss, then to the stone. It was clear to Carolina that she wanted to know what they meant.

Carolina placed Lyddy down on the moss and put her china hands around the stone to pour out tea; then she put the bit of bark to her lips and pretended to drink from it. She helped Lyddy to drink from her cup and poured a cup for their visitor. The Indian girl understood the game and soon began playing tea party, taking her turn at pouring and offering.

After a while she stretched her hands toward Carolina with the first finger of her left hand alongside the first finger of her right hand. She indicated that one finger stood for Carolina and the other for herself. She pretended to draw the fingers apart, but they would not come. Carolina decided that the gesture must mean that they would play many such games together. She laughed and nodded, then made the same sign.

The Indian girl gathered together several twigs and began to arrange them in a pattern on the moss. She found pieces of bark, which she stood up like tepees. She hollowed out a place that by her actions of pretending to be burned was surely a fire where cooking was being done. The twigs now being placed around the fire were braves and women, and some smaller twigs were children. Carolina nodded and laughed as she watched the story being told her. Then, by a tepee, two twigs were placed. One, that was small, was to represent the Indian girl herself, for every time she touched it she pointed to herself

until Carolina understood. The taller one must be her father, not her mother, for the girl had fastened bits of grass to certain sticks to indicate women with long hair.

Carolina nodded.

The Indian girl took the larger twig in one hand and, holding it up, crooked one of her fingers over its head. She was telling Carolina what her father was, but Carolina could not understand what the sign meant. She shook her head slowly. The sign was repeated, but Carolina only shook her head.

Then Carolina gathered twigs and bark to make a representation of the wagon encampment. After it had been assembled, animals and all, she pointed to one particular wagon with her father and mother and Mark sitting by their fire.

The Indian girl clapped her hands and laughed, a gurgling sound that made Carolina laugh with her. She held out her doll to show how she was made from a piece of buffalo hide with a bit of the tail for hair; beads were sewn on to make the features of a face and a tiny feather had been tucked into the beaded headpiece. It was coarsely made. It smelled and felt greasy. It was stiff and unyielding. Carolina examined it politely. Secretly she was glad that it was not hers to love.

Then she held Lyddy toward the Indian girl and showed her how Lyddy was made with her china face and hands and neat little feet, the sawdust-stuffed body that made her so flexible. She drew her hands over the blue dress with its tiny button, scarlet sash, and trim tucks; then she turned the skirt up

ever so little so the Indian girl might peek under it and see the white petticoat and the pantaloons edged with lace.

The Indian child laughed and clapped her hands, then she bowed her head up and down in admiration.

They exchanged dolls, and Carolina cradled the one of buffalo hide while the dainty New England doll was held in sturdy embrace. Carolina started to croon one of the songs she often used to send Lydia-Lou to sleep, and the little Indian girl followed her example. But her voice did not sound like singing — it sounded like creek water slipping over stones; it sounded like wind through the scattered sage bushes on the prairie; it sounded like rain drumming on a tepee or antelopes skimming over open lands. It sounded like many things, Carolina thought, but it did not sound like music.

The sharp ears of the Indian girl heard something, and she ceased her song-making. She looked up into the space before her, listening. Then Carolina heard it — the beating on the bucket that was Annah Putnam's dinner bell.

"I must go now. Mama's calling me to come," Carolina said. She stood up quickly, placed the hide doll on the moss beside her mother, and reached for Lyddy.

The Indian child shook her head and held Lyddy against her buckskin tunic.

"No, no! You must give me back my Lyddy!" But the words were meaningless.

The Indian held Lyddy close to her heart and indicated that Carolina should do the same with the doll of buffalo hide.

Carolina stamped her foot on the moss. The next moment she would have kicked the hide doll into the underbrush in spite of the pleading look in the black eyes.

The beating on the bucket sounded again, coming through the stillness of the little green room. Carolina heard her father calling her name. She dropped to her knees on the moss and held out her empty arms, mute in their entreaty.

"Car — o — lina! Dinnertime. Car — o — lina!"

Back of her name and through it and far more insistent were the words so often on her father's lips: "Pioneer folk must be willing to share."

Slowly she nodded her head. Slowly she reached out to pick up the doll that lay on the moss. Slowly she held it to her heart, placed her lips against its tress of buffalo hair, and nodded.

The other child watched every move, understood, and bent her lips to Lyddy's china face. Then she laid Lyddy across her knees and made a series of swift, imperative gestures.

First she picked up the long twig by the tepee and crooked her finger over it. She placed it beside Lyddy and put her two hands close together, fingertips pointing toward Carolina. She opened her hands wide as she stretched them before her till her arms reached their full length, smiling as she did so. She repeated the gestures, but Carolina only shook her head. The Indian girl made one of her gurgling happy sounds, picked up Lyddy, and held her close to her heart.

Carolina got up, turned away quickly, and pushed through the low-hanging branches of the little green room to the path that ran beside the creek. She stumbled and fell, for it was often hard to see, but she never lost her hold on the Indian doll. She wanted to sit down and cry, but there were more reasons than one why she could not do that.

"I'm c-coming, Papa," she called, "I'm coming — q-quick as I can."

Before she got to the encampment, she knelt down by the creek to wet her eyes and cool their burning. When she stood up, there was Lyddy's brown dress where she had left it stretched on a bush to dry. It was dry now; the wind had ironed it well and it was ready for Lyddy to wear again, but Carolina left it where it was, hoping the Indian girl would find it tomorrow. She had no use for it now.

Tucking the hide doll inside her dress, Carolina ran swiftly over the path and toward the Putnam wagon. Up the steps and into the wagon she disappeared for a moment; then she joined her family sitting by their fire. Her father looked at her and smiled, forgiving her lateness now that she was with them.

"You had to tuck your Lyddy into bed first, didn't you?" he asked.

Carolina nodded.

Mark had caught a fine string of fish, and they were sizzling in the iron skillet. Annah began to put them out on the wooden plates. "Two apiece tonight," she said, "and some sallet I found alongside the creek. That's a meal to do us all good."

Carolina had not thought she could eat, but with food on a plate before her she discovered that she was hungry. Eating eased the ache within her, and she bent her head over her plate.

"Cat got your tongue?" her father asked.

Annah said: "She's tired. She's been playing with the other children and it's made her sleepy. Look at the way she's nodding over her food! Carolina, you'd best go to your bed in the wagon. I'll be in to tuck you up as soon as we've finished."

Carolina stood up and went toward the wagon. She fumbled up the steps and into the comforting darkness.

Chapter six

IT WAS NOT long before Annah got up from the fire and went toward the wagon. John Putnam and his son picked up the buckets and started toward the creek to get their evening supply of water. They had gone half of the short distance when a sudden muffled scream could be heard coming from the wagon. They stood in their tracks; then, because no further sound followed the scream, John Putnam feared the worst had happened. Wagon folk had told him that every now and then an Indian, with thieving intent, crept into a wagon and when caught in the act would kill sooner than be discovered. It was strange that this should happen at an encampment, but evening had come down and darkness could be cover for any deed.

"Stay where you are, Mark, but keep your eyes on me. If I don't come out of the wagon by the time you count ten, get help."

"Your gun, Pa?"

"It's stowed in the wagon."

John Putnam, his arms swinging freely, fingers tensed, strode back toward the wagon. To run might excite someone in the camp and there was no need to do that — yet. When he reached the steps by the opening, he saw Annah standing there. Her face was pale and tight as the drawn canvas; her hands were clinging to the wooden frame.

"Annah, what is it?" he asked, his voice just loud enough to reach her. "An Indian?"

"No, oh no," Annah moaned. "It's Lyddy — she's gone!"

"Lyddy!" he gasped, then turned to face Mark. He could just see the boy, standing still as a tree, a bucket hanging from each hand. "Go on and get the water," he called; then he sprang up the steps and into the wagon.

Annah grasped his hand. There was light in the wagon, for she had lighted the candle in the tin lantern and hung it from the center hook. She pointed to Carolina, sleeping soundly among her quilts. Held in her arms, and pressed as close to her as Lyddy had ever been, was a small piece of animal hide with a tail of hair down its back. A few beads were sewn on it in haphazard fashion. It had a strong greasy smell.

"What is it? Where did she get it? Where's her Lyddy?" Annah spoke fast. Bewildered herself, and angered, she expected her husband to have answers for the thoughts that vexed her.

John sat down on the slat-back chair and put his head in his hands. The shock of utter relief made him laugh, but he tried to smother the sound so that he would not wake his daughter.

"Oh, Annah, Annah, I thought there was an Indian in the wagon and that harm had been done! Had you screamed twice, I would have roused the camp to battle."

"Well, it is an Indian of sorts. An effigy of one. And it's dirty! The whole wagon stinks. I'll have to take Carolina to the creek first thing in the morning to wash the smell off her. Where did she get such a horrid object?"

"That's what I'm wondering."

"I'm taking it from her, John, and I'll thank you if you'll take it and burn it in the fire." Annah reached down and put her hand on the hide bundle.

But even in her sleep Carolina's hold on it was tight.

"Let it be, Annah, for a while. Go out and sit by the fire. Perhaps Mark has come back with the water. Tell him what's happened."

"But what *has* happened? That's what I want to know. Carolina goes off to play with her Lydia-Lou and she comes back with a mess of leather. That's why she was so quiet at supper!"

"Go out and sit, Annah. I'll be with you and Mark when I've done some thinking."

As soon as John Putnam was alone with the sleeping Carolina, he moved over and sat on the quilt beside her. With fingers strong enough to draw milk from a cow's full udder and sensitive enough to strip the udder dry, he took the strange object in his hand and gently eased it away from Carolina. She slept undisturbed.

He turned it in his hands, trying to decide what it was and what it meant. It was an Indian artifact, of that he was sure, and it was well made for fingers that did not readily turn to small manufactures. It had some value, for the beads sewn on it were the kind largely used as a medium of exchange. A tiny feather, perhaps from a hummingbird, had been tucked into the headpiece; small as it was, it might have the significance of eagle feathers.

It was a doll: that was certain; but could it have belonged to the daughter of a chief? The feather might be the indication.

It had been greatly loved: that too was certain. The fact that it was dirty and grease-laden meant that where its owner had gone the doll had gone too; what she had eaten her doll had shared.

Carolina stirred and reached her hand across the quilt. Moving her fingers in search of something they could not find aroused her. She opened her eyes. At first they were too filled with sleep for her to see anything; then gradually they cleared and focused on her father. He was sitting near enough for her to reach out and touch him and he was holding something in his hands. She stared at it; then slowly her eyes filled with tears that spilled soundlessly down her cheeks.

"You have another doll, Carolina. Do you want to tell me how you got it?" He put his hands around her thin body and lifted her up to his lap.

She put her arms around his neck and buried her face against his shoulder until her eyes had dried and her voice could be steady; but her voice never got louder than a whisper as she told her father what had happened and described with her hands the signs the Indian girl had made, both those that Carolina understood and those that were meaningless.

"Will I ever see Lyddy again, Papa?"

"No, Carolina, I think you will not; but if I've learned anything about Indian signs, I think that we shall see our land in safety."

Carolina blinked. Her lips moved, but no sound came.

"Your Indian friend was trying to tell you, Carolina, that her father is a chief; that crooking of the finger over the head is the sign for chief. Of course, I do not know for sure, but I think that what she was telling you at the end by opening her hands and holding out her arms before her was that her father would see that you — and your family — would go on your way without molestation."

Carolina nodded. She took up the doll from where it lay on the quilt and studied it carefully. "What shall we call her, Papa?"

"Shall we call her Safe-Conduct? You'll see how well the name suits her before another day's journey is behind us."

"That's hard to say, Papa, and it doesn't slip over my tongue the way Lydia-Lou did, and I don't think I can make up any songs to it."

"Safety is not an easy thing to gain, little daughter, but it's what pioneering folk need to get their homes established."

"I'm sleepy, Papa."

He eased her down into the bedding and drew the quilt up to her chin. "Want that I should introduce your new doll to Mama and to Mark?"

"Yes, Papa, if — if you'll put her back in my arms again. I wouldn't want her to be lonely on this first night away from her familiar home."

"I'll do that, Carolina, and now good night. I'm thinking that by another night the wagon wheels may have come to rest on our own land." When he leaned over to kiss her, she was asleep.

A few moments later he joined the others by the fire. The Indian doll was in his hands.

Annah looked up at him expectantly. "Nothing but embers left, John, but that thing will burn well, it's so heavy with grease."

"We're not burning this, Annah, not now or ever."

"John!" she gasped. "You mean you're not going to throw that stinking bundle in the fire?"

He shook his head.

"Where's Carolina's Lyddy, Pa?" Mark asked. "Want that I should go and look for it along the creek where Carolina was playing?"

"No, son, you'd not find it. Lyddy's asleep tonight in some Indian hogan. Like as not she's in a little girl's arms the way her doll was in Carolina's and will be as soon as I return it. I'm thinking that we'll none of us ever see Lyddy again."

Annah drew in her breath quickly. "I don't know what Carolina is going to say."

"Carolina has already said it. She made her decision when she parted with Lyddy this afternoon and accepted this doll in trade."

"But, John, she loved Lyddy so! Sometimes I think she loved her more than her own life."

"But perhaps not more than all our lives, Annah. This doll

is our safe-conduct. Unless my notions are very wrong, I think it's an Indian pledge that we'll go the next day's journey with clear passage."

Annah stared at her husband. Love was in her eyes, but there was awe in her face. "How do you know?"

"Carolina has been telling me what took place this afternoon, and I've been interpreting, that's all."

"But, John, *how can you be so sure?*"

"There are some signs, Annah, that can always be understood. We'll be on our way in the morning, not at sunup but soon after, so the other wagon folk can follow in our lead."

"You mean," Mark said, half in surprise, half in excitement, "that we're going ahead without an interpreter?"

"We have one." John Putnam touched the Indian doll lightly with his finger, then turned toward the wagon. Going in, he placed it on the quilt beside Carolina where her hands would find it in the morning.

Annah followed him. "But the smell, John —"

"We'll have it with us for a long time, Annah, and we'll be thanking God for it."

It did not take Mark long to roll up in a blanket by the fire. Like one of the animals, he knew enough to get rest when he could. But before John Putnam joined his son, he had gone to each one of the eleven wagons at the encampment. To each one he told his story and said that his wagon would be rolling in the morning. Many of the men who had gained knowledge of

Indian ways agreed with his interpretation of his daughter's play with the Indian girl, and there was not one who was unwilling to follow in the wake of the Putnams.

"We'll be at the land office to get our claims by tomorrow night," one man said.

"Some of us may even be camping on our own land," John Putnam answered.

Next morning Carolina took Safe-Conduct down to the creek when she went to wash. She stood her beside her when she ate her first early meal. In everything, she did with her what she had once done with Lydia-Lou. After the oxen were yoked and the wagon was ready to roll, John Putnam lifted Carolina to the front seat and told her to hold Safe-Conduct on her knees.

"What if she gets tired and wants to sleep, Papa?"

"You can cradle her in your arms for a while, but when we see Indians approaching let her stand on your knees so they can salute her. Safe-Conduct is the daughter of the daughter of a chief, and they'll want to know that all is well with her."

There were bustle and excitement among the wagon folk at the encampment as animals were brought in from grazing, yoked or hitched, whichever the case might be, to their wagons, and a readying was made for departure.

John Putnam cracked his whip in the air. It split the hubbub like a pistol shot. His oxen moved forward. "Catch up!" he shouted to the others, some of whom were almost ready.

"We're a-coming!" they shouted back.

"We'll soon be on our way!"

"Take an hour's rest at nooning, and we'll be even with you!"

Women leaned from their wagon openings and waved kerchiefs or bedding. Boys beat on buckets, or skillets that had not yet been packed. The four little girls with whom Carolina had played held up their dolls — wood, rag, corn husks, china — and let them wave to the small but important personage who stood between Carolina Putnam's knees.

The oxen splashed through the creek, then settled into their slow plodding pace on the broad plain that led toward the valley of the Platte. The path was deeply rutted, for many wagons had gone this way to the settlement a few short miles ahead. It was hard pulling, for the land rose steadily, and nowhere in it was there a sign of life.

During the first hour they saw no more than a few buffalo grazing in the distance and a small herd of antelope; then a band of Indians came down from the hills. Swift on their light horses, they circled the Putnam wagon widely, saluted it, then divided their numbers. Three on one side, three on another, they kept pace with the wagon, long enough for the Putnams to see the gestures they were making as the Indians pointed ahead and clapped their hands; then they raced away and disappeared into the hills from which they had come. At different times during the day they, or other Pawnees, appeared and went through the same actions. They smiled now as they clapped their hands and made sounds that, meaningless as they seemed, could yet be understood.

John and Annah Putnam, walking beside the oxen, waved to the Indian scouts and pointed ahead. They held their hands to their hearts, then stretched their arms out before them.

"Will they know we're saying that our hearts are homing?" Annah asked.

"They'll know our intent," John answered. He glanced back at Carolina. Upright on her knees the doll was held. "She's giving us safe-conduct."

Mark sat on the wagon seat, blowing experimentally on a new willow whistle and talking with his sister.

As the wagon lurched forward and up into the hills, Carolina turned to have one last glance back. Framed in the canvas opening, she saw the land they had come through as once she had seen the New Hampshire land when they left it. Then she saw a small white village with a church spire pointing upward, the whole held between green hills as if God were holding it in the hollow of His hand. Now she saw a flat and waiting land, laced with slow-moving creeks. Spread wide on the palm of God's open hand, it looked ready to welcome those who had journeyed far to reach it.

"How soon now, Papa?" she called ahead to him.

"Over this next rise of land, Carolina, soon now, very soon."

3 1172 01035 5345
D.C. PUBLIC LIBRARY